Farm-mouse Fairy Tales

Mice and Forest Friends Tales from My Gettysburg Farmhouse

Shirl Knobloch

Farm-mouse Fairy Tales: Mice and Forest Friends Tales from My Gettysburg Farmhouse

Edited by: Jennifer Sabatelli

Cover Art by: Shirl Knobloch

ISBN 13: 979-8-234-01855-7

• • •

Also By Shirl Knobloch:

Birdsong, Barks, and Banter: Adventures of an Animal Intuitive Reiki Master and Her Home of Misfit Companions

The Returning Ones: A Medium's Memoirs

You're Never Too Old for Fairy Tales

Reenactments from My Heart: Spiritual and Supernatural Civil War Fiction and Poetry

Once Upon a Fairy Tale

Strength of a Lion, Soul of a Lamb: A Collection of Wolfhound Fairy Tales and Poetry

My Ten Legged Journey: The Road to Rainbow Bridge

Waiting for the Next Village Attack: Growing Up Italian, a Jersey Girl Reminisces

Enchanted: Fairy Tales for Young and Old

The Voice of Their Hearts: Learning Animal Communication

• • •

Remembering the Magick: Fairy Tales for Those Lost, Found, or Wandering

By Salt Water: Tales of the Sea

Spirit Whispers: A Collection of Ghostly Fairy Tales

Yes, I Knit Blankets for Squirrels: A Fairy Tale Author and Her Bushy-Tailed Friends

Not All Witches Are Cruel, Not All Fairy Princesses Are Kind: A Collection of Witch Fairy Tales

Being Different: A Guide for Young Empathic Mediums

Lore from Lavender Lane: Woodland Fairy Tales

The Briar, the Bramble, and the Rose

The Pilgrimage: A Collection of Soul Tales

Nantucket: The True North of My Heart

When One Song Ends: Birdsong, Barks, and Banter II

• • •

Between the Moon and Magick: A Collection of Fairy Tales

Winter Tales

Ever After: Fairy Tales of Love

• • •

They say that by the time you are about five years old, you already have forged your path and direction in life. Well, as a little girl, I stuck my head out of my bedroom window and sang to the birds. I did this until the neighbor next door "caught me" and commented on how lovely my song was—and my shy nature held those notes in until I became an animal communicator many, many years later.

So, I guess it's true. The soul speaks to you at a very young age, telling you your future. This book is dedicated to all who sing: the birds through sun and storms; the little mice whose song can only be heard by others of their kind; and the ocean giants, whose whale songs travel the depths.

May all who read my stories find their notes again, long hidden within the soul, and rekindle the passions their young hearts always knew.

Dedicated to my children and grandchildren,

who share my love of reading

• • •

• • •

Table of Contents

Wings of Silk	1
Henry	9
Fireflies Never Lie	13
The Dress Competition	17
Black as Night	21
The Dream Catcher	25
Wishes and Magick	29
Star Stories	33
Wallace's Flowers	37
Pierre's Folly	43
The High Ground of Kindness	47
Treasures	55
Witch Burrs	61
Things Can Turn	67
Jasper's Tree	71
Just Look at the Sky	77
Hats and Homes	83

• • •

The Lantern 89

Mourning and Fire 97

The Book Witch 103

Wild Horses 107

Stories and Time 111

• • •

Wings of Silk

Thimble was a tiny mouse fairy. She was as tiny as a thimble, but she was a brave explorer. She loved to fly throughout the forest, day and night, in search of adventures. But she would only go to the edge of the woodland, where the farmer's field bordered the trees.

One day, however, Thimble flew into some netting that the farmer had placed around his garden and caught her wings. She tried and tried to free herself, but in the process, one of her wings was torn. She could not fly.

The world is a dangerous place for a teeny fairy who cannot fly. Thimble crept into the bushes and quietly wept. She was a long way from home; no one would know where she was. Her tiny mouse paws would never make the journey home. She wept for hours, and the sun set in the sky as night fell on the forest.

Suddenly, Thimble heard a "*hoo, hoo*" coming from the trees.

"Who is crying?"

Thimble looked up and saw a big barn owl. Now, owls are not friends of mice, and so Thimble started quivering.

"Do not be afraid," the owl hooted. "I am Hephzibah, Guardian of the Woods. I *protect* all who live here, not harm them."

Thimble squeakily sobbed and told Hephzibah her story. Hephzibah flew down from the tree, extended her wing, and told Thimble to climb on. Together, they soared through the night sky, the wind tousling Thimble's soft fur. Hephzibah soared high above the farmer's fields, high above the barn she called home, and back toward the dense woods.

"Here, this is where I live," Thimble squeaked. Hephzibah's sharp eyes spied the tiny mound on the forest floor. She softly placed her wing to the ground so Thimble could climb down.

Thimble took her tiny paw and placed it on Hephzibah's beak. "Thank you," she whispered. "I will never forget your kindness." Hephzibah hooted farewell and spread her wings in the night sky.

Thimble wept as she tried to spread her broken wing, but her efforts were futile. She went home to the fairy village and felt all the pity of her fairy siblings.

"What will you do, Thimble?" they squeaked. "A fairy must fly. Without wings, you are just an ordinary mouse."

Thimble did not sleep that night. Her broken wing was very sore, and her mouse tears dampened her tiny pillow. She crept outside with the morning sun and looked forlornly at the blue sky.

Soon, a robin tweeted, “What is wrong, little mouse?”

“I am a fairy,” Thimble squeaked.

“A fairy?” the robin chirped. “Then where are your wings?”

Thimble’s broken wing lay folded against her back. “They are broken,” she cried.

“Oh my,” chirped Robin, “oh my, indeed. I must be on my way—there are worms to catch. Would you like a ride?”

And with one swooping motion, the robin spread her wings and let Thimble climb aboard her back. Together, they soared above the trees, the sunlight warming Thimble’s face and drying all the wet spots from her tears. “Don’t cry, Thimble,” said Robin. “I can come and get you every morning with the sun, and we can fly together.”

And so they did. The two became inseparable friends. The robin’s chirp awakened the little mouse with the sun, and off they went on adventures together.

The other fairy mice envied Thimble. Robin could carry Thimble farther than any of their wings could manage. On top of that, Robin always sought out the nicest fruit and berries for Thimble to eat.

Thimble and Robin spent spring and summer together and felt the coming breeze of autumn on their faces.

"The leaves are starting to turn," Robin chirped. "Soon, I must go."

"Please don't go!" Thimble cried.

"I must. Winter is too cold for me. There will be no worms to catch, and I have no cozy fairy mound nest to keep me warm."

Robin had grown to love the little mouse, and though she knew what she had to do, she was worried for her friend. How would Thimble fly and be safe without her?

"Come with me," Robin suggested to her friend.

But Thimble was always taught not to leave the fairy mound and the surrounding woodland. There were no fairies or fairy mounds where Robin was headed, just a frightening landscape for a little, wingless mouse.

Robin had already stayed longer than she should have; farmers were already gathering the harvest. In a heap by the farmer's vegetable garden patch, she spotted the netting that had broken Thimble's wing. A thought came to her. With her beak, she cut and cut and tore off a tiny piece of netting. Holding it in her beak, she flew back to the fairy mound and gave it to Thimble.

"Thimble, you must be very brave and go to the cave at the edge of the forest. There, the spiders live. They know how to spin spider silk and weave creations. Maybe they can fix your wing."

Now Thimble had not ventured out at night since she had broken her wing. "I am afraid," she squeaked.

"Don't be scared," Robin chirped. "I will ask my friend to protect you on your way.

"Who is your friend?" Thimble asked.

"Hephzibah," Robin answered.

Thimble's mouse eyes widened. "I know Hephzibah!" she squeaked.

Robin chirped excitedly, knowing her friend would be well cared for in the forest. "I will tell Hephzibah to come for you tonight," she sang as she flew off into the sky. "I love you, Thimble. I will see you in the spring."

Thimble tried to hold back tears, but she cried as she watched the speck of wings disappear in the distance.

That night, as promised, Thimble heard a familiar "hoo, hoo" in the darkness. The whoosh of a large wing caused her mouse ears to wiggle.

"Climb on, we have a long journey ahead of us," Hephzibah hooted.

Under the moon and under the stars, the tiny mouse and the magnificent owl journeyed. They came to a dark cave, a place where the spiders lived.

Thimble placed the tiny piece of netting she held in her paws on the cave floor in front of the spiders. "Can you help me?" she squeaked.

Hephzibah hooted, "I wish for your best spinner and weaver to come forward."

The spiders knew of Hephzibah. She was the queen of the woodland, and whatever she wished must be obeyed. A tiny brown spider crept in front of the others. "I am the master spinner. How may I serve my Queen?"

Thimble slowly tried to spread her broken wing. "Ouch!" she squeaked.

"I see," said the spider with all of his glowing, yellow eyes. His hairy legs picked up the piece of netting. Slowly, he began to weave an intricate lace, attaching it to Thimble's injured wing. Into the night he labored, spinning fine threads while Hephzibah looked on from a tall stalagmite in the cave.

When beams of morning sunlight broke through the cave's opening, the spider tore off the last silky thread and bowed to his queen.

"Good as new," he whispered in spider language, (which Hephzibah understood, for she spoke all the languages of the woodland beings).

"Thank you," she hooted.

Thimble slowly stretched her wings wide and felt them expand on the breeze. "My fairy wings are back!" she squeaked with delight.

"Come, Thimble," screeched Hephzibah, "it is time for us to leave. I do not like the sunlight. It is far too hard on my night vision eyes."

Off they flew, Hephzibah bidding farewell to the little mouse as she headed toward the farmer's barn roof. "Safe flight home, Thimble," she hooted.

When Thimble returned home, the other fairy mice were amazed, touching and complimenting her beautiful, new wings. *"My, they are soft as silk."* *"Look how they glisten."* They all squeaked with envy.

Thimble thought proudly to herself, *I am no ordinary mouse. I am the most beautiful of fairies.*

Thimble flew each morning, all through the autumn crispness and all through the snowy, wintry skies. Her strong wings carried her swiftly through the sky. During each flight, she searched and searched, hoping to see a black pair of wings on the horizon.

One spring morning, a familiar chirp filled the air. Thimble ran out from the fairy mound, spread her wings, and took to the sky. Alongside, the familiar wings of Robin glided through the breeze.

"That's a lovely pair of wings, my friend," Robin sang.

And Thimble squeaked with loving delight as the two of them flew on their way, for there were worms to catch and berries to eat and stories to be told by both.

Henry

Once upon a time, there lived a tiny mouse named Henry. Henry was a country mouse; he lived in a tiny hole in a log, in a crawlspace of a farmhouse surrounded by fields and wildflowers.

Henry loved flowers. His whiskers always twitched when the wind captured the fragrance of the violets and wild roses. But Henry's favorite flower was the dandelion. He loved the soft yellow petals that smiled like the sun, and he loved the fluffy clocks that sent seeds flying in the wind, carrying wishes to the moon.

Henry loved to sleep inside the clocks; he was extremely tiny and not much weight, so dandelions provided the perfect bed on lazy spring evenings. When he woke, Henry would give out a big yawn and send dandelion seeds soaring through the air each morning.

"I wonder where you fly," he squeaked. "Maybe some of you will make it to the moon," he whispered to himself.

Henry loved to gaze up at the moon and twinkling stars. Some mice said the moon was made of cheese. Henry liked that idea. He loved cheese.

Each night, Henry found a soft bed among the dandelions, and each morning, he wished upon the seeds as they flew high into the morning sky.

One night, Henry thought he heard a soft voice call out his name. "Henry," it whispered.

Henry thought he was dreaming, so he shut his eyes and tried to drift back to sleep.

"Henry," it called.

Henry opened his beautiful, black eyes and saw a tiny fairy hovering by his dandelion bed. She was even tinier than he was, with wings that shimmered in the moonlight.

"I am the dandelion fairy," she spoke with a lilting voice. "I send the seeds on their journey, some near and some very far," she whispered. "I hear you wish upon them every morning. You may only see me at night, for in the morning, I become invisible to man and mouse."

"The moon is very far away," she continued, "even for a dandelion fairy. My seeds cannot make it that far. But they can make it high up in the sky. Would you like to see me send some there? Most humans hate my beautiful dandelions, but I know you love them, Henry, so I will grant you a very special wish. I will give you the magic to send them on their journey, too."

Henry's ears spread wide, his whiskers twitched, and his mouse body shivered all over with excitement.

"Now, blow your wishes on the wind. Tell the seeds where to fly."

Henry took a deep breath. He blew as hard as his tiny mouse lungs allowed. The seeds took flight in the air, going higher and higher and higher. Henry watched as tiny points of light twinkled in the sky. Each had become a new star, a star for a tiny mouse to wish upon in the darkness.

The fairy's wings fluttered. "I have to go now, Henry," she whispered. "It is nearly morning. You did an excellent job. You have sent these babies to a very special place. Thank you." And with a whoosh of the breeze, she was gone.

Each night thereafter, Henry sent special wishes and love to the stars. And when his final sleep came, the dandelion fairy came to take his body to the stars to be with them.

Fireflies Never Lie

Once upon a time, there lived a gentle elephant who loved to gaze up at the night sky and watch the stars. The grasslands, his home, were very dark at night, and the stars filled the sky with brilliance. He would trumpet with his trunk, lifting it toward the heavens, and try to reach the stars.

How I wish I could reach one, he thought to himself. *I would hold it in my trunk and light the darkness.* You see, he was a baby still, and darkness was a frightening place. He had no friends except for the stars above, who shone down upon his sleepy eyes until he drifted off to slumber.

One night, he came upon a peaceful valley at dusk. *The stars are just waking up*, he thought. Then, he saw a burst of light ahead, then another, and another. Soon, hundreds of bursts of light grew stronger as the sun lowered her head. The little elephant ran towards them and captured one on his trunk.

"Are you a star?" he trumpeted loudly.

"Hey, that hurts my ears! A star? Are you crazy?? I am a firefly. Harold's the name. What's yours?"

"I.....I don't know my name," the little elephant softly answered.

"Well, I will call you Noisy, because you are."

"What does noisy mean?"

"It means LOUD!!" the firefly screamed. But the little elephant only heard a whisper from his tiny friend.

"Why did you think I was a star?" Harold asked.

"I love stars. Each night, I raise my trunk and try to hold one. They are my friends who light the scary darkness," Noisy answered.

Now Harold might seem brusque, but he had a very kind firefly heart. "I will be your friend and your nightlight. Lie down and close your eyes." With that, Harold flashed his light several times and called some friends to help. Together, they shone a glimmer around Noisy as he peacefully started snoring.

"Yep, Noisy is the right name!" Harold muttered.

The other fireflies flew off to do their firefly "stuff," but Harold stayed all night with Noisy. In the morning, when the little elephant awoke, he found his friend sleeping on his trunk.

"Harold, wake up!"

Harold opened his tired eyes. "I must be off now, Noisy. But don't worry, I will find you again when the sun lowers her head at dusk." With a tiny glimmer of light, Harold was off into the brightening sky.

True to his word, because fireflies never lie, Harold found Noisy as the sun set in the western sky.

• • •

Noisy lifted his trunk.

"Don't do it!! Are you trying to make me deaf?" exclaimed Harold.

"Sorry," Noisy whispered, sheepishly lowering his trunk.

The two spent this and many more nights together. One morning, however, Harold lingered a bit longer with his friend.

"Noisy, I won't be coming back tonight."

"Why not?" the elephant cried.

"I feel the change. My wings are getting weaker, and my light is getting very dim. It is my time to leave."

"But you told me you would be my friend, and you said fireflies never lie."

"Sometimes, we must leave, even though we don't want to go. Do you remember your mom?" Harold asked.

"Bad men came in the dark. I HATE the dark!" the elephant screamed.

Suddenly, the tiny firefly felt his face become very wet as his heart filled with sorrow. "Look up at the sky, Noisy. I will be one of those stars, shining for you. When you see one twinkle, it is me. I will always be your nightlight." Harold looked into the watery eyes of his friend one last time and slowly flew away.

That night, Noisy waited and hoped. Harold didn't come. The sun would be setting soon; it would be dark, and he would be all alone again.

Just then, he thought he heard a tiny whisper. *No, never alone.* Noisy looked up at the stars. He saw one very bright one twinkling.

"Harold, is that you?"

Noisy lifted his trunk up to the sky and let out a very loud trumpet.

"Sorry, Harold," he whispered. And he fell asleep.

The Dress Competition

June came in with scorching heat this year, but all the little beings knew work had to be done. It was time for the summer gala—and, of course, the best ballgown competition.

The stakes were high; competition was fierce. The spiders flew in from all across the forest. The silkworms rested their little mouths so they could be proficient chewers to spin the softest silk. The fairies posted little flyers on mushrooms, looking for the best seamstresses in the woodlands.

The competition preliminaries selected three final entrants. Judges took their positions quite seriously; they were sequestered in the trunk of a huge redwood tree during the finals. Judge Greene, a dapper grasshopper, always had a serious expression, giving no clues as to who had the strongest lead. Judge Butter, a monarch, was very fair, always giving newcomers to the competition an equal shot at the prize. And what a prize it was! A week-long vacation at the Fairy Mound Resort, all nectars, seeds, and worms included in the package.

Suzie Spider wanted that prize. She was tired from raising all eighty of her children last month. She needed a break, and her eight legs were killing her from all her mothering spider tasks.

In competition with Suzie were Betty, Bessie, and Bea, the silkworm triplets. They had five wins under their silk belts and were looking for the sixth.

But all eyes—and Suzie had four pairs of them—were on the strange newcomer, a tiny fairy named Elisa. She carried a little sewing basket, a tiny thimble, and a silver needle in a pouch.

Elisa smiled at her fellow contestants. Suzie Spider sneered, and the silkworm triplets shrugged their shoulders.

Soon, the judges rang the starting bluebell. They had two days to complete their gowns. They could use the provided thin slices of birch bark to cut out their patterns, but all other materials had to be gathered or created by them.

Suzie started furiously spinning intricate designs out of webs. But her legs ached; sometimes, she dropped a stitch and had to start a corner all over again.

The silkworms' mouths grew tired. They had stayed up late the night before, chewing and crunching delicious party snacks. It didn't look good for this trio.

But where was Elisa? She had vanished in the leaves, searching for just the right materials. She found what she was looking for—a patch of fluffy dandelions.

Elisa took out her silver needle and slowly began weaving the soft seeds and fluff into a lovely design. She was very nimble with her thread and soon had enough material to cut out her birch bark pattern. She created a simple design. Her creation would be a flowing shift of softness that swayed in the breeze.

"Hmmph!" screeched Suzie, looking at the crooked corners of her hem.

Meanwhile, the silkworm triplets just turned down the corners of their tired mouths. Their gown was incomplete; it had an entire side panel missing.

The judges rang the ending bluebell.

"Not your best work," chirped Judge Greene as he hopped alongside Suzie's entry.

"This work is incomplete!" Judge Butter buzzed as he flew by the silkworm triplets in a huff. "No incomplete work is acceptable in our contest. You know better than this!"

Then, the judges came to Elisa's entry. The soft gown fluttered in the breeze, soft as a feather and sewed together expertly.

"My, this is beautiful," sighed Judge Greene.

"My wife would love this," Judge Butter gushed.

"We have a winner!!" they chimed in unison. Elisa beamed and proudly accepted her vacation certificate.

A week's stay at the Fairy Mound Resort—well, that wasn't exactly the prize Elisa had hoped to win. You see, her family owned the Fairy Mound Resort. She could have her fill of nectars and seeds and spa treatments any day of the week.

"Judge Greene, Judge Butter, I have a request. It seems Suzie Spider could sure use a vacation and a spa treatment for her tired legs. And the silkworm triplets could rest their mouths on my family's delicious nectar smoothies. May I give my prize to them?"

Suzie's eight eyes nearly popped out of her spider head. The silkworm triplets' mouths dropped several inches.

"This is most unusual," Judge Greene chirped.

"Oh, loosen up, Greene," Judge Butter buzzed in a high voice. "Let's let the winner decide. And, er....might I discuss the option of buying that gown for Mrs. Butter? Our milkweed anniversary, number three, is coming up soon."

Elisa smiled and handed the dress over to Judge Butter. "What better anniversary gift than a dress full of wishes," she whispered. "Take it."

True to her word, Elisa gifted her prize to the other contestants. The spider and the silkworms had the time of their lives at the Fairy Mound Resort. Elisa was given the week off by her parents so she could join in on the fun with her new friends.

"I wonder what next year's prize will be?" she smiled and whispered quietly to herself.

Black as Night

Once upon a time, in a land of dragons and castles, there lived a little crow named Ren. Ren loved the forests, the rivers, the flowers that covered the woodland floor, and the tall, ancient trees. And Ren was dearly loved by his family.

But something always clouded the little crow's eyes from seeing the world with happiness. You see, he loved colors. All the colors of the flowers, all the colors of the leaves, all the shades of green in the forest, too many to count. All these colors caused longing in his heart, perhaps because Ren's feathers were black, a deep, dark shade of the darkest black.

"Why can't we have beautiful feathers like all the other birds?" Ren asked his mother.

"Why, I think you are the most beautiful of them all, Ren," she crowed lovingly.

"I hate my feathers. I love red and green and yellow and blue, all the colors of the rainbow, none of which are black," he answered.

Ren's mother didn't know what to do to make her son realize how handsome he truly was. His feathers gleamed in the sunlight with beautiful iridescence. But Ren didn't feel beautiful. He often flew off by himself, not wanting to talk with any of the other crows.

One day, a strong wind carried Ren very far, much farther than he had ever traveled. He lost direction; he could not find his way home.

"Caw, caw," he cried. But his mother could not hear him.

Then, a loud hoot sounded from a nearby tree. "Who comes this way?" asked the booming voice.

"It is me, Ren," he whispered.

"You aren't from this part of the forest. What are you doing out by yourself? It's nearly dark, and you have woken me up a bit early this evening."

"I am lost," the little crow answered.

"Why did you fly so far from home?" the owl asked.

"Because I am ugly. My feathers aren't red or blue or yellow like the other birds."

"Well, my feathers are brown, and I think I am very handsome," hooted the owl. "Don't you realize how special your feathers are, my little one? See, here in the darkness, you can hide. Not everyone here is a friend like me. And look—see how your feathers shine in the moonlight with all the colors of the rainbow?"

"The rainbow?" exclaimed Ren. "My feathers are like a rainbow?"

"Yes," answered the owl. "You are a very special bird. Red birds are red, bluebirds are blue, yellow birds are yellow. But you shine like a rainbow in the sun and moonlight."

Ren's dark eyes shone with tears. Not tears of sorrow, but tears of happiness. For a moment, he forgot he was lost and so far from home.

Suddenly, he heard a loud chorus of caws in the sky. Mama had gathered all her friends to search for her little boy.

"Here, Mama, I am here with my friend...."

But the owl was gone.

"Mama, I am a rainbow," the little crow cried.

"Yes, my darling. You are *my* rainbow," cawed his mama, wrapping her loving wings around him.

And from that moment on, little Ren realized he was a handsome black crow.

Leon was a little mouse. But more than that, he was a dream catcher. Leon came from a long line of dream catchers. From the time of his great-great-great-great-great Uncle Morris to his father, RJ Mouse, Leon was destined to carry the mantle of dream catcher for all the children of his mouse village.

There were lots of bad dreams. Dreams of big dogs, mischievous cats, and traps that snapped and could catch a tiny paw in the wink of a little mouse eye. These images could frighten a young mouse wide awake in the night.

So, each night, Leon carried a tiny lamp and visited all the young mice in their tiny beds and soothed them to sleep with a fairy tale or lullaby song. He carried the feather of a bluebird in his coat pocket and touched it to every little mouse's whisker, calming them into sound sleep. For he was a dream catcher; he carried off any bad dreams lingering in the darkness.

Now, Leon hardly slept himself. He was so busy traveling from nest to nest, mouse baby to mouse baby. When morning came, he would be all tuckered out and tried to get a few snores in before it was time to go back to work. But Leon was having trouble sleeping. It seems no one came to catch his dreams, and the darkness carried many fears and shadows for a tiny mouse.

Soon, Leon began falling asleep while collecting seeds. His friends saw him catching his head as it drooped, and they noted his startled, tired eyes opening with a start.

"What's wrong?" they asked worriedly.

"I am not sleeping well. And I am having bad dreams."

"Well, that's new. The dream catcher not sleeping? Take some time off, Leon," they urged.

"No, I must see that all the children sleep soundly. I am the dream catcher, like my father, and his father, and his father before him."

Leon had eased many a night for his friends, letting them catch up on needed rest while their infants slept soundly in bed (thanks to his stories and songs). His friends did not forget.

"It's time we return the favor," they squeaked. "But how? What should we do?"

"Leon once told me an old legend," one of the mice whispered. "He said it was made for very bad dreams. We must gather bits of twine and feathers. We will need help. We need to make a circle and hang these feathers with the colorful seeds and nuts and little trinkets we all have hidden away," he added.

"What are they for?" the mice squeaked.

"It's for a dream catcher, to trap all the bad dreams while you sleep. Mice in other villages—ones without someone like Leon—use them to soothe their babies. We need to make one for Leon."

Arthur Mouse, a gifted artist, sketched out a design from the imaginations of Leon's friends. All the mice went home in search of bits of yarn and feathers and beads, found in the forest and on the outskirts of the human village. Clara Mouse, a gifted seamstress, was given the task of stringing them all together. By nightfall, it was finished.

Leon left at dusk to make his dream catcher rounds. He sang a lullaby to Holly Mouse, and he read five fairy tales to the Woodmouse twins. He then crept back to his nest, exhausted. As his paw searched for his lamp switch, he spotted it.

Hanging from a little hook above his bed hung the dream catcher. It was beautiful! Colored glass beads and soft feathers, held together with twine, stood encased in a grapevine circle wreath. The glass beads caught the lamplight and twinkled like stars.

A tiny note lay on his pillow:

For Leon,

For all the bad dreams captured by you each night. For every song, for every fairy tale, for every peaceful night's slumber.

Signed,

Your friends

Leon was overcome. His head had barely touched the pillow when the sound of a little dream catcher's snores filled the room. No more bad dreams—not when he had the most beautiful dream catcher in the world above his head.

Wishes and Magick

Once upon a time, there lived a beautiful little princess. She was dearly loved by her parents, but she had no friends her own age. Her nanny would sit and tell her fairy tales about kingdoms far away among the stars. Each night, she would look out the castle tower window, up into the night sky, and wish for a friend to visit from one of those kingdoms in the stars. She would choose the brightest star, reach her finger toward it, and make a wish.

Each night, she would wish. But no one came. She loved her nanny, but she could not run through the castle gardens and sit among the pretty flowers with her. Her nanny's knees ached, and her bones were old and tired. So, they would sit on a garden bench, and the nanny would tell her story after story until the castle cook called them in for lunch each afternoon.

Now, the castle cook was a wise old woman. Something about the cook made the princess feel safe to confide in her, to share these nightly wishes.

"Sometimes," the cook whispered, "star wishes are not very far away. Sometimes, they are very close."

"What do you mean?" the princess asked.

"Do not stop wishing. You must believe in magick," the wise woman answered.

So that night, the princess looked out her tower window and found the brightest star. Again, she wished for a friend.

The next morning, no one came. She dressed and went outside with her nanny again and sat at the garden bench. The little princess told her what the cook had said.

"Don't listen to her gibberish," scolded the nanny. "Leave her to her pots and pans and pastries."

When lunch came, the little princess was exceptionally quiet.

"What is wrong, princess?" asked the cook.

"Nanny says you talk gib....gib....." she whispered.

"Gibberish! Is that what she said? Well, we will just have to teach that old crow a thing or two about wishes and magick!" she giggled.

That night, a beautiful full moon lit up the sky. The princess looked out her window and asked the stars once again to bring her a friend. Someone to play with, to share secrets with in the grass, to love. "Oh, please send me that someone," she cried.

Suddenly, she heard a strange chattering sound from the trees. A little black bird swooped down upon the window ledge. His beautiful feathers shone like iridescence in the moonlight. And upon his back, hundreds of tiny stars were scattered.

"You are so beautiful!" the princess cried. She gently scooped him up in her hands and carried him inside. He quietly chattered until the princess fell asleep, and when morning came, the little bird gently poked her cheek with his beak.

When the nanny came to take the princess outside, she was not too thrilled to see this bird in her bed chamber. "What is that dirty thing doing in here!!" she screamed. "Fetch the servant. Tell him to get a broom and chase this thing out!"

"No!" the princess cried. "He is my friend. I am not going to the garden bench today. My friend and I are going to play together in the tall grass."

And so they did. The beautiful little bird flew alongside as the princess ran. He pecked at the grass seeds as she sat amidst the flowers. She counted the beautiful stars on his back and told him how she had wished upon each one.

The nanny went to the king and said it was one or the other.....either she or the bird had to go. The princess and her new friend watched as the nanny walked toward the castle gates, tapestry bag in hand.

Soon, the cook rang the bell for lunch. The little princess sat at one end of the table. A beautiful black bird sat at the other, pecking bits of bread and figs. The cook's eyes sparkled with laughter. As the sun hit her face, the little princess swore she could see stars in them.

Star Stories

Once upon a time, in a dense woodland forest, there lived a mama bunny and her little daughter. Each night, the mama would hold her daughter's paw as they sat outside and gazed at the stars.

"Tell me their stories, Mama," the little bunny would ask. And mama bunny told a story about each and every twinkling star until the little bunny's eyes grew heavy, and her bunny ears started to fold over in drowsiness. Then, mama bunny would gently carry her back to her den.

The little bunny learned to do all the things a bunny needs to know—how to keep a clean den, how to make a nourishing meal, and how to sew and knit warm woolens for when the snows came. One day, she would grow and have a baby of her own to love and share star stories with each night.

Mama bunny was an expert seamstress. She often stitched little dolls for her daughter. She quilted a warm coverlet for their bed to snuggle under each night. And she showed her baby how to sew beginning stitches on a piece of cloth with a porcupine needle and spider silk for thread.

Each night, after her baby went to sleep, mama bunny would sit under the moonlight and stitch a treasure for her little one. And with the rising sun, she would hide it away in the tree trunk chest papa bunny had made long ago, before he went in search of food one night and didn't return.

The baby bunny asked, "Where's Papa?" Mama bunny only twitched her runny nose and wiped her eyes with her apron. "Some stories are not happy," she would only whisper.

"I want to hear each one," the baby bunny cried. "Every star's story in the sky, Mama. And Papa's, too. Please tell me."

So that night, mama bunny told her daughter of the dangers of the woods, the bad things that could happen in the night. But she also told her never to be afraid to look up at the stars in the darkness and remember all the bright stories of life, those bright as the stars.

"Papa would be so proud of you," she whispered. "You have grown to be such a wonderful daughter. And you have learned all that I have tried to teach you. One day, you must use all that knowledge when I join Papa once again."

"Where is Papa? Is he in the stars?" the little bunny asked.

"Perhaps he is," mama bunny smiled. "Perhaps his story continues in another woodland, where he is waiting for us. But, for now, let us sit beneath the stars and treasure this time together."

The little bunny grew. She grew more beautiful each day, and soon, male bunnies came courting at their den door.

Mama bunny was tired. Her eyes were weak, and she had only a few more stitches to complete her surprise gift. She worked tirelessly into the night, until her paws ached and her shoulders hurt from hunching over the cloth.

Then the night came when it was finally finished. Each tiny spider-silk stitch was expertly woven into a cloth of love. Mama laid her work across the tree trunk chest and kissed her daughter on the cheek as she slept.

"Goodbye, little one. It is time for me to go off alone. Soon, I will see your papa's face in the stars."

When her daughter awoke the next morning, she found a beautiful dress. In glittering spider silk, hundreds of tiny stars sparkled in the morning sun. A little note lay by the dress. It read:

> *Remember all our stories, all our stars. Tell them to your daughter and think of me and Papa watching from above. It is my time to leave. Always remember how much I love you.*

The little bunny clutched the dress to her heart. It was so beautiful. She wore it on her wedding day. Soon, there would be little ones to tell a sky full of stories to in the night. Some would be sad, like when Mama and Papa left. But life is filled with stories, good and bad. One just has to look for the brightest stars in the night to remember the happy ones.

Wallace's Flowers

Once upon a time, a little hedgehog named Wallace lived among a tiny patch of woodland. Wildflowers dotted the village lanes that skirted the woodland. Each morning at sunrise, the little hedgehog wandered the patches of wildflowers, selecting the prettiest blooms. Then, he would make his daily visits to the aging beings that lived in the woods.

First stop was Jane the Badger's den. She had been homebound since a bad fall last winter on the ice. Wallace left a tiny bunch of bluebells at her door. Then, Henrietta Robin, who was nest-bound because of a wing injury, waited for her morning bouquet of thistles and violets.

All who lived in the woodlands knew Wallace. He had a smile and a friendly hello for all along his route. They called him the "postman of flowers."

Just like the village post, no weather stopped Wallace. In times of storms, he would don his galoshes and happily stomp through the puddles along the way. In snow, instead of blooms, he cut boughs of evergreen and holly to brighten the doors and nests of friends. Part mailman, part nurse, but wholly a trusted friend, Wallace was loved by all.

One summer morning, Wallace didn't come by Jane's den. Worried, she shouted out to Harmon Hare, who lived next door. "Something's wrong, Harmon," she cried. "Wallace hasn't come."

Harmon told her not to worry, but his long whiskers twitched in the breeze with anxious thoughts. He set out hopping to find his friend.

"Have you seen Wallace?" he asked Clayton Crow.

Clayton cawed *no* and shook his beak. "I will get the rest of the crows to search," he answered.

Soon, word spread all along the woodland, and everyone started looking for their friend.

The crows found him. It seems poor Wallace had been struck by a car early in the dawn hours. A kind man, seeing that the hedgehog was still alive, carried him to the local wildlife rehabilitation center in the village. The crows saw Wallace resting in an outdoor pen.

He looked pretty banged up. He had a bandage around his paw, and part of his fur had been shaved where medicine flowed through a needle into his body.

"Caw, caw," the crows cried. But Wallace didn't stir. He just lay there, still. The crows came back with their findings to the woodland creatures.

"Oh, no," cried Jane the Badger. Henrietta Robin was beside herself with grief. Harmon Hare's whiskers drooped in worry.

"We have to do something!" Jane cried. She could not leave her den, but Jane started creating flyers for Harmon Hare to post on all the trees and den doors. *Help Wallace,* they read. *He was always here to cheer us up. Now, it's our turn to repay his kindness.*

The next morning at sunrise, a group of badgers, hares, crows, and squirrels formed an unlikely pack with a purpose. They trudged out along the village lane to make a bouquet. They gathered bluebells, thistles, wildflowers, ivy, and violets. Harmon Hare pulled out one of his long whiskers and tied the flowers into a small bouquet.

"Clayton, take this to Wallace for us."

Clayton took the small bouquet in his feet and set flight across the lane. It was too early for the rehab center to open. Wallace still dozed in his pen. Clayton cawed, causing Wallace to stir and open a sleepy eye. Then Clayton placed the bouquet at the door to Wallace's pen. Wallace smiled with his eyes, for he didn't have strength to talk yet.

When the rehab center opened, a worker went to check on Wallace. "What is this? What in the world? It seems you have an admirer, old man. Someone left you flowers." The worker smiled. "Probably just blew with the wind during the night," he whispered to himself.

The next morning, the scene repeated. Little beings foraging for flowers, a crow making a delivery, a rehab center worker finding another bouquet.

"Now this is really strange," the worker muttered. "Two bouquets, two days in a row."

Wallace grew stronger. Soon, he was sitting up, and the horrible needle was taken out of his paw.

"Looks like you are finally going home," the worker said the next morning, as he picked up yet another bouquet on the ground by Wallace's pen. "Hurry up and join that lady friend of yours who keeps bringing you flowers."

Two days later, Wallace was well enough to go home. Happiest of all was Harmon Hare, for he was running out of whiskers to tie the bouquets. Clayton Crow watched the whole event and reported back to Jane and her friends. Flying home, he cawed, "Wallace is coming home!!!"

When Wallace reached his den, a bouquet of wildflowers greeted him, with a little note attached:

Now, it's our turn to take care of you. Rest up. Don't worry about us. There will be time enough for you to collect flowers once again. For now, just get well and accept the gifts we bring in gratitude.

For the next month, flowers, soup, nuts, seeds, and whatever delicacies Jane could think up were delivered each morning and placed at the hedgehog's door.

The rehab center put up a little ceramic sign (with painted flowers and a little painted hedgehog) at the pen where Wallace recovered. They would never forget how a little patient received get-well flowers every morning.

Pierre's Folly

Once upon a time, in the French countryside, there lived a tiny mouse called Pierre. Pierre lived in the cellar of a large house, surrounded by acres and acres of grapevines. The owner of the house was a winemaker, and Pierre lived among the ancient wine barrels and learned all about the master of the house's trade.

Pierre dreamed of being a winemaker, too. All the mice loved grapes. They would squash them with their tiny feet and make delicious grape juice. But no one knew about this thing called wine and why people came from all over to purchase the bottles in the winemaker's shop.

Pierre watched the winemaker and learned each step of his winemaking process. Pierre resolved to make his own wine someday. He would have his own vineyard, and mice would come from miles around to fill tiny glass bottles with his special creation. He would become famous.

First, Pierre commissioned Francois, the mouse village carpenter, to make him a tiny oak barrel. When the barrel was finished, Pierre and his friends rolled it into the wine cellar and chewed off a spigot on one of the winemaker's largest barrels. They let the wine drip into Pierre's oak barrel and then rolled it off into Pierre's mouse hole. Pierre let the barrel age and permitted no one to touch it until the wine was ready.

Finally, Pierre announced that his wine would be ready to drink that night. The excited mice squeaked out word to all the mice around the countryside. Word spread through squeaks that Pierre had created a new drink, only tasted before by humans. "Come and taste wine!" they squeaked.

The mice came from all across the countryside to the party. They shared tiny goblets of this strange libation. It tasted like squashed grapes, but different. Some loved it. Some hated it and spit it out on the ground, making horrible mouse squeals of disgust. "This tastes rotten," they squeaked. Pierre said that they had "no taste." Each imbiber called him the new village winemaker and raised goblet after goblet to him.

But then, something happened. The mice started swaying. They started seeing four eyes in front of them (instead of two) in the faces of their friends. Their squeaks started to slur.

"What is happening?" cried the ones who had spit out the strange juice.

"It's the wine! It's making them sick."

One of the disenchanted customers said, "They are all going to die! I told him it was rotten!!!"

Frantic, the mice called Raquel Rat, who knew all kinds of healing ways. She had a forest apothecary shop and knew how to concoct all kinds of medicinal potions and salves.

"What happened here?" Raquel asked. The mice told her about Pierre's juice. "Oh, I see," she smiled. "They aren't dying, they are drunk," she squeaked with a smile. "Best to leave this wine juice to humans," she added. "Nothing good will come from it. Tell Pierre I want to see him right now."

"We can't," they squeaked. They pointed their paws over to the corner where Pierre lay, passed out on the cellar floor.

"Quick," Raquel ordered. "Everyone who is able, help me get all these mice to safety before the humans find them."

Pierre slept for the next day. His friends all complained of terrible headaches after the party. No one wanted any more wine juice. From then on, only fresh-squeezed grapes filled tiny mouse goblets.

Pierre's short-lived days as a winemaker quickly came to an end. But Pierre's quest in the beverage field remained undeterred.

"Perhaps there is some kind of juice I can make with those juniper berries that grow in the forest," he whispered to himself. *"I heard some humans picking them and talking about a drink called gin. I wonder what gin is,"* he squeaked.

"I will follow them and see how to make it for my next party. Maybe Raquel knows what ingredients to add......."

Poor Pierre—he was in for a scolding from one very wise old rat.

The High Ground of Kindness

Simon was a baby rat. He was a domestic rat, with beautiful black and white fur. He was born in a pet shop in a big city. Both his mama and papa had been sold, but Simon remained behind.

One night, the sound of a loud crash and broken glass woke him from slumber. Two large shadows loomed by the front of the store, and the sound of cages being overturned frightened the tiny boy. All at once, he found himself on the pet shop floor, his cage door opened. Simon ran and ran. He hid in the corner until all was quiet again.

When morning came, Simon looked around. The shop was a mess! Glass aquariums were shattered, and cages where puppies and kittens once slept were now empty. His body was trembling with fright. The large snakes had been freed, as well. Simon found a crack in the wall, squeezed through, and ran and ran until he came to a large tunnel underneath the shop.

Soon, he found other rats. But they weren't like him. Their fur was different, their faces meaner. They weren't kind to Simon.

"Look, it's one of those 'highfalutin' pet shop rats," they squeaked.

"Yeah, the kind that think they are better than us," another rat chimed in.

"Look at those designer spots!" cried another. "Too good for the tunnels, aren't you? Scram!!"

Simon scurried off, so tiny and afraid. He ran through the dirty tunnels for hours until his little paws were sore and his fur was matted and covered in dirt and grime.

Then, a voice squeaked out. "Hey, what's your name? Boy, you sure are stinky, even for a rat."

"My name is S....." Simon started to answer, but then he replied, "Stinky, that's my name."

"Well, it sure fits. C'mon, me and the gang found some pizza in the tunnel. Wanna join us?"

Simon didn't know what pizza was, but he was so hungry and tired that he followed the rat. The pizza was delicious. Better yet, the other rats were friendly, admiring his stink.

"My mom sure wouldn't let me get this stinky," one squeaked. "She makes me wash up every night. She keeps saying that upstairs humans think rats are dirty, so we have to show them we aren't."

"I don't have a mom," Stinky squeaked. "I don't have a home."

“Well, you can stay with us,” the rats squeaked in unison. “Just don’t come over to my house,” one rat cried. “My mom will have a fit!!”

So, “Stinky” stayed. He made sure his fur was always covered in grime. He avoided water at all costs, which was hard to do in the tunnels that led to the sewers. It was too important; the others must never know his secret.

Stinky made quite a name for himself among the rats. Soon, he became the alpha. The tiny munchkin had grown into a strong, dominant male. No one challenged him for the role of leadership. He led with a strong, kind paw, and everyone loved and respected his word. When fights arose among the rat clan, it was Stinky who settled them. When choice pieces of pizza or other treats were found, it was Stinky who divided them equally among the families.

That is, until he met Cecilia. She was beautiful. She had the softest fur, the pinkest nose, and the longest whiskers. It was love at first sight. Well, at first sight for Stinky. Cecilia twitched her nose at the lovely scent wafting off her suitor’s fur.

“If you want to court me, you have to take a bath……er……many baths,” she squealed. “Ew….is that a piece of mozzarella cheese sticking to your tummy?”

“Why, thanks,” squeaked Stinky, placing the tasty morsel in his teeth.

Although he had managed to keep his true identity a secret for so long, Stinky came to realize that he had no choice. Either he revealed his secret or he would lose the love of his life.

One night, he asked Cecilia to meet him by the sewer tunnel. There was something about this stinky rat that made Cecilia accept this strange date, and she went. As the moonlight shone down from the sewer grate, Stinky dove in the water and bathed his fur. As the dirt and grime washed off, beautiful black and white fur emerged.

Cecilia squeaked, "Your fur! You are one of the upstairs rats!"

"Yes," Stinky answered. "My real name is Simon. I had to hide my fur so others down here would accept me. Please do not tell anyone, Cecilia. I don't want to be alone."

Cecilia's deep, black eyes glistened with tears. "I won't tell," she whispered, and she placed a rat kiss on Simon's forehead. "Now, let's stink you up again." And she proceeded to help rub grime and mud once again into his fur.

The two became a couple. But Cecilia insisted on a once-a-week sewer bath tryst under the moonlight for the two of them.

Soon, Cecilia was expecting. Simon was very worried about how the babies might look.

"We might have to run away," he told Cecilia.

"I know. I will follow you anywhere," she squeaked. "I love you, Simon."

The babies soon arrived. All, thankfully, were covered in deep dark fur. That is, except for one, a little girl with a tiny tuft of white on her forehead that formed the shape of a star. She was Simon's princess. "I shall call you Princess Star," he squeaked with love.

And she was his princess. He fawned over her and showered her with kisses. Though she wrinkled her nose up at her father's unique scent, Star loved him equally as much. She loved her daddy with her whole rat heart.

None of the children knew their father's secret. Cecilia brought it up to Simon occasionally. "But what will happen when they grow and have children of their own? What if......"

"We will worry about that if it happens," Simon would reply. "Look, all of them are fine. Everyone loves Star's little star. Don't worry, Cecilia."

That spring, heavy rains came to the upstairs land. Water seeped into the tunnels, and the levels grew higher each day. Soon, torrents of water came down, forming currents that flooded the sewers.

The rats were all scurrying to find dry ground. Cecilia and Simon were gathering up the children and running for their lives when a strong current whisked little Star away. The whole rat clan watched in horror as Simon dove into the water and swam after her. When the pair emerged from the water, the clan squealed.

"Your fur!!!" they shrieked. "You are not one of us. You are one of THEM!!" they cried.

Simon took his shaking daughter back to her waiting mother's arms. The rest of his children gazed upon their father's fur.

"Come, we will explain everything," Cecilia whispered as she shielded her children from the judging eyes of the rat clan.

Most of the onlookers squeaked with cries of, "Banish them!" The rivals for Simon's leadership role urged the throng of rats to rid the tunnels of this imposter. But out from the holes of the tunnel walls came a few dissenting voices.

"I am Lawrence. When I lost my leg in a trap, it was Stinky who saw that my family was fed." The old rat hobbled with a twig crutch. "If he goes, I go with him." Lawrence slowly joined the little family.

"I am Juniper," squeaked a one-eyed, skinny rat. "When all of you had no use for a half-blind rat, it was Stinky who always showed me kindness. If he goes, so do I."

Soon, several of the rats shifted their positions and scurried over to the banished rat family.

“Let them all go,” the rival clan squeaked. “Look at them, a band of misfits—one blind, one crippled, some stragglers. Less mouths to feed, and more pizza for us!” they cheered.

And so, the little band of weary travelers, led by one tired (but clean) black and white rat emerged through the tunnels to a place of higher, dry ground.

As for the others, well, the rains continued for the next week. The tunnels flooded; there was no escape.

Treasures

Hermie was a tiny mouse who lived about one hundred years ago in the garment district of New York City. Now, Hermie knew clothes. At a fast glance, as he raced by the feet of New Yorkers, he could look at a human and tell which tailor cut the cloth, who sewed the hems, and where the buttons came from.

Hermie loved to sleep among all the remnants of soft, warm cloth in the garment factory during cold winter evenings, and he often took snippets for all the new mouse moms so they could line their babies' nests. He carried off red and green buttons at Christmastime and delivered them to mouse homes to be used for holiday decorations. All the mice in Hermie's tenement never went without warm coats and blankets, for the caring mouse always took what would never be missed by human eyes. All the tiny pieces too small to do anything with—but just perfect for little mouse bodies—found their way into a little box Hermie kept outside his mouse den labeled *"Free for Those in Need."*

Hermie was dearly loved. Mother mice would bring their little ones to see him, smartly dressed in tweed jackets and calico pinafores. A specific type of cloth needed? A special occasion coming up? *Just ask Hermie*, the mice knew, and he could deliver. Thanks to Hermie, snippets of lace adorned tiny wedding veils, and many a black, silk bow tie adorned the tiny necks of nervous mouse grooms.

Over time, Hermie learned to create patterns, and his paws became just as skilled as the nimble hands on any New York City tailor. His small fingers could create delicate details more precise than any human hand.

One day, an elderly couple came to Hermie's door. They pulled a tiny wagon filled with bits of cloth, flannels, calicos, silks, and scraps that Hermie vaguely recognized, though from many prior mouse seasons.

"We know you are the best tailor in the entire mouse world," the white-whiskered gentlemouse squeaked as he held his wife's paw in his. "My wife has kept all these snippets from our babies and grandbabies—from each Christmas, each wedding, and each new baby celebration. And we owe these all to you."

The gentlemouse continued, "We are old, and we don't have much time left here. We don't have much money, but we can give all that we have. We want to leave something special for our family, something for them to remember all the special moments we shared together. Can you create something, maybe a warm blanket, with all these pieces? Something to hold each new baby that we cannot hold in our own paws?"

And with that, the gentlemouse handed Hermie a tiny bag of pennies. "We've been collecting these for years. It isn't much, but it is all yours."

Hermie took the bag and shook the mouse's paw. "I will do my best," he squeaked.

Hermie worked each night by the streetlamp that shone through the window of the empty garment shop. He used the bits of thread that lay in clumps by silent sewing machines. He climbed up onto a long table and laid out all the pieces of cloth, carefully stitching them together by hand until the first rays of morning light. Then, he carefully folded up his work, hid it inside a crack in the wall, and went home to have a bite to eat. He would get some rest until night came. Then he would return to his worktable.

This continued for many nights until Hermie was finished. A beautiful quilt lay on the sewing table. Hermie didn't know the name, but he created something that human hands had been stitching for many, many generations to preserve family memories. There was a patch of white lace that had once been part of a blushing bride's gown. There was a patch of cozy, worn flannel that had once kept a tiny mouse warm in her cradle. Each tiny stitch was fashioned with such skill that they were hardly visible between the fabric seams. Hermie carefully folded his creation and carried it home in his paws.

The next morning, he knocked on the elderly couple's door. When he placed the quilt before them, the couple squeaked with happiness. "Thank you, Hermie!" they cried. "It is so beautiful."

"Look, Papa!" the woman cried. "Why, it's Lucy's wedding gown. And here, Martin's old school jacket. And here, my calico cooking apron." The woman could not stop crying and squeaking and pointing to each and every square.

The man shook Hermie's paw and thanked him again. "Are you sure we gave you enough?" he asked.

"You gave me more than enough," Hermie whispered with a smile. "You gave me back all my memories, too. I remember each and every square, each piece of fabric left on the garment shop floor, waiting for a home." With that, Hermie squeaked goodbye and left before the mouse couple caught the tear forming in his eye.

When the mother mouse lifted the beautiful quilt to put it in her wooden hope chest, there was a tiny lump in the back of the fabric. A skilled mouse had sewn a little pocket in the quilt corner. Inside was a cache of pennies, another type of treasure collected through the years.

And one day, if excavators tear down the walls of an old New York City tenement, they might see a bundled scrap of old cloth and throw it in the rubbish pile. Some don't know treasure from trash. But generations of mice knew, thanks to a tailor named Hermie.

Witch Burrs

Once upon a time, in a forest woodland, there lived a hedgehog couple. They were filled with excitement; the couple was expecting their first little babies in the spring. Papa took excellent care of his wife, and when the time for the birthing arrived, he excitedly told all the other woodland beings the news. Three little hedgehogs were born, one boy and two girls.

Mama and Papa were over the moon with joy. But as the days passed, they realized something was not right with their son. The two girls had begun sprouting little quills, but the boy's body remained soft, not spiky.

"Give it time. He will grow." Mama tried to ease the worry in her husband's face, although she was worried, too. You see, hedgehogs need quills to protect themselves; without them, their little son Arnold would be an easy target for enemies in the forest.

Days passed, and all the animals of the woodland village stopped by with presents to see the babies. "My, how adorable!" they gushed when the two little girls, Bea and Bess, popped their heads out of their cradles. But no one said anything when poor little Arnold—with a bald little head and a body soft as down feathers—peeked out.

"Poor Sid and Sally," they whispered. "Such a heartache. What will they do? They can't keep him locked up inside. What a shame. What a shame."

From the trees, the crows watched and listened to the whispers. They were wise crows and knew the dangers of the forest, especially for hedgehogs without quills. They cawed amongst themselves and wondered what they might do to help. Sid and Sally had always been kind to the crows, sharing bits of food during the harsh winter. And crows never forget kindness.

"Caw," one said. "Let's collect sharp evergreen needles and bring them to the fairies. They can sew a coat for Arnold."

"Caw, caw," one answered. "Evergreen needles get dry and brittle; they won't make a fine coat."

"How about sharp twigs and rose thorns?" another cawed.

"Caw," another replied, "thorns are sharp enough, but the stems will dry and crack. Let's go ask the fairies for help."

So, the crows flew high above the trees to the edge of the forest where the fairies lived. The fairies knew all the woodland beings. They had attended Sid and Sally's wedding. When they learned news of the births, they were filled with joy. But then, the crows told them about Arnold.

"Oh no," they whispered. "We must find Esme."

Esme was a kind witch who lived in a small, secluded thatch hut by the lake. Only those who knew their way through the deepest woods could reach her home. Esme knew all the plants and beings of the woodlands and was kind to all. When one was ill, it was Esme who came with herbal potions and salves to tame raging fevers and to splint broken paws.

"Esme will know what to do," the fairies chanted, and off they flew. The crows cawed in thankfulness and returned to the tree above the hedgehog's burrow.

Esme heard the news and thought. Then, she smiled. "Here," she said as she brought down a large jar of witch burrs from a shelf filled with herbs and salves.

Now, witch burrs are the seeds of the sweet gum tree. If you have never seen them, they are sharp and spiky to the touch and never lose their hardness. Kind witches keep them for healing and luck.

Esme told the fairies not to worry. She packed them little treats for their long flight home and assured them that she would help.

She got out her needle and twine and began winding and tying the witch burrs together, sewing them onto a soft piece of flannel. It took her most of the night to finish, her tired witch eyes and hands working in the dim light of her beeswax candles.

The next morning, she folded up the witch burr cape, placed it in a burlap bag, and fastened it to the back of her loyal wolfhound, GreyBear. Together, they took off on the long walk back to the woodland glen where the hedgehogs lived.

The crows were the first to spot the pair as they walked down the path. The witch's walking stick made tapping sounds on the ground as GreyBear's long tail swished back and forth along the hedgerows. When they came to the hedgehog couple's den, the wolfhound softly barked his greeting. Everyone knew GreyBear; he was a kind wolfhound. He even let the crows pick tufts of fur from his head for their nests.

Sid and Sally opened their door, and out flew the two little hedgehog girls. "Bea, Bess, this is Esme."

Esme smiled and said, "I hear there's another little one, a boy." She grinned.

"Yes, but we don't let him outside. You see, he has no quills," they answered.

"I know. The crows told the fairies, and the fairies told me." Esme unpacked the bundle from GreyBear's back. "I think this might help. Now, let me see that special little boy."

When Arnold peeked his soft head outside the den, Esme chuckled. "Now, you are certainly special. My, a hedgehog with no quills, how about that? But guess what? I have something here in my bag that will fix all that."

Esme opened the burlap bag and showed Arnold a handsome witch burr cape. "Tie this around your neck and under your tummy," she told the little boy.

Arnold tied his witch burr cape snugly around his middle. The soft flannel underside was soothing to Arnold's fragile skin. The spikes were a sharp and protective barrier against enemies.

"Wow!" his sisters squealed.

"Caw, caw, caw!!" the crows cackled in the trees.

"Look, Mama, Papa," said Arnold. "I have spiky quills!!!"

Mama and Papa hugged their son……carefully.

And over time, Arnold grew to become the most handsome hedgehog of the woodland. With each growth spurt, Esme added more witch burrs to cover his tummy and back. The kind witch became his godmother, always keeping a special place in her heart for the handsome, witch burr boy.

Things Can Turn

Theodora had the gift. Her mother had it, her grandmother had it, and all the female rats of her family possessed *the sight*. Theodora could see things. Other rats came to her burrow to know their futures. *Who will I marry? Will I have fifty babies or one hundred?*

Theodora could also see spirits. Rats seeking solace would ask her to reach out to family members on the other side. Being a seer, though, is dangerous. Theodora's mother had warned her—everyone loves you when all is well, but when things take a turn, it is you they will blame. "Oh, Mama," Theodora responded, "that won't happen. They are all my friends."

But it did happen. One night, Theodora's mother was forced out of bed. Young Theodora cried and cried for her, but she never answered, and she never came back home again.

Theodora's home was in the back of an old general store. Many rat families also lived in the walls. There was ample food to be found, in burlap sacks that strong rat teeth could easily chew apart. There was dried corn and grains and sugar and seeds for planting. It was an easy life, and Theodora lived happily for several years. She never used her gifts for harm, and she only told the other rats wonderful news from her visions.

However, one day in a vision, Theodora saw something horrible. The shopkeeper was sprinkling something over one of the piles of seeds. He was grinning and whispering to his shop assistant, "This will fix those rats. We'll get each and every one!!!"

Theodora shook with fright. "Mama," she cried. "Please tell me what to do."

Soon, the translucent body of a rat shimmered near Theodora's head. "Remember what I warned, child. Things can change," she squeaked. "Don't be part of this. Please leave this place, my child!"

But Theodora loved this place. Her friends were here. She had helped so many young rats find their true mates and assisted in so many births.

"Mama, you are wrong. I have to tell them."

And so, she did.

"You're lying, Theodora," the other rats said. "You just want those seeds for yourself. You know they are the tastiest. Why, you are just like that no-good mother of yours, a witch!" they screamed.

Theodora was heartbroken. She went inside her burrow and cried for days.

Then, a pounding on her den door came in the middle of the night. "Theodora, Theodora, help us!!" they cried. "Our babies are dying. Many elders are sick. Help us!!"

Theodora shook her head. "I tried to warn you. It is the seeds. You would not listen. There is nothing I can do." With that, she closed her den door and sat in the darkness.

In the stillness, Theodora heard a voice in her head saying, "I warned you, my child. They will come, just like they came for me." Sure enough, it was then that Theodora began to hear shouting outside her door.

"She's a witch, just like her mother!" they squeaked. "She cursed those seeds out of spite. She is killing our babies!"

The voices grew louder and louder. Then came the pounding on her door again. They dragged Theodora from her bed and tossed her in the alley in back of the general store. "Don't ever show your ugly witch face around here again!!!" they screamed.

Theodora was heartbroken. Her heart held only kindness and love for all of them. Now she knew what had happened to her mom.

Any other rat in Theodora's position might have turned her back on all her "family." But Theodora was different. Theodora only had goodness in her heart. She waited until all the voices died down and all the rat families were back in their burrows, tending to the sick. She then crept inside the wall of the store and found what was left of the tainted seeds. One by one, she carried each seed to the patch of dirt beside the alley, burying them in a large hole she dug with her sharp paws.

When there was only one seed left, Theodora carried it in her mouth and went to a dark corner of the alley behind boxes of trash. With teary eyes, she bit down on the seed.

"Come, Theodora. It's time to go home now."

"I am coming, Mama," she softly squeaked, as her broken heart shed its final tear.

When the rats woke the next morning, they went to their favorite bag and found it empty. "That spiteful witch came and took the last of the seeds. Now what will we feed our sick babies?"

If only they had listened, things might have turned out differently.

Jasper's Tree

Jasper was a tiny mouse who loved pockets. His mom made all his clothes with love. His overalls had huge front pockets—almost as big as he was—on every pair.

Jasper loved collecting, and he put those pockets to good use. His eyes sought the best rocks, pinecones, leaves, and seeds. Any bit of trash or shiny wrapper always found its way into Jasper's paws and pockets.

One day, Jasper found a shiny rock that sparkled in the sun. He had never found one like it before. It was a treasure.

"Look, Mom, we are rich!" he squeaked when he got home. "Look what I found. I think it's a fairy treasure."

Now, the fairies don't take kindly to those who steal their treasures. And it just so happened that a large diamond was lost in the woodlands that morning by one of their own.

Word spread around the mice village about Jasper's find. Elders came to inspect the treasure; indeed, they said, it must belong to the fairies.

"Put it back, Jasper! Never take from the fairies. They will seek revenge on our village if you don't return it."

Jasper forlornly picked up his treasure, placed it in his overalls, and trekked back to the site where he found it. This time, on the very spot where it had been, he found a shining, golden seed pod.

"Wow!" squeaked Jasper. "This is a treasure trove!" Forgetting that he still had the diamond in his pocket, Jasper picked up the seed pod and scurried home.

"Did you get rid of it?" his mom asked.

"Er....I forgot," squeaked Jasper.

"You forgot!?!" his mom cried. "What will I tell the elders? Oh my, they will banish us from our home!"

Soon, a knock came upon the door, and three white-bearded mice called out for Jasper.

"Have you left it where you found it, son?"

Jasper squeaked a soft, "Yes," his whiskers twitching with fright.

"Good. Who knows what would have become of us if you had not returned it? Good night," they squeaked and left.

Jasper's mom squeaked with dismay, "You are bringing that treasure back at first light tomorrow morning. I don't want you picking up a single thing in that forest. Do you hear me, Jasper?"

"Yes, Mom," he squeaked.

"Now get some rest. I am waking you up with the birds in the morning."

During the night, a strange thing happened. The golden seed pod burst wide open, and a tiny golden fairy stepped out. Now, the fairy had been sent to wreak havoc on the entire mice village, but she was a kind fairy. Jasper was just a little boy, not a treasure hunter. So, she decided to give him a chance to place the fairy treasure back on his own. Back into the seed pod she crept, waiting to see if this little mouse would do the right thing.

The next morning, Jasper headed off to the woodlands, both diamond and seed pod in the pocket of his overalls. When he got to the special site, a group of tiny fairies was waiting in the trees, hidden from sight.

For one last time, Jasper looked longingly at the diamond. He then placed it on the patch of moss where he had first glimpsed its sparkle. Next, he reached for the seed pod and placed it on a nearby leaf.

Suddenly, the seed pod opened and out jumped the fairy. "Thank you for returning what is ours," she said.

"Yes, thank you," echoed a chorus of tiny voices in the trees.

"In gratitude, we will give you something in return." The golden fairy held out an old, worn, tattered bag. She placed the raffia bag with a drawstring closure in Jasper's paws.

"This is no ordinary bag, Jasper," she whispered. "It has been woven by the fairies and is filled with magick."

Jasper loved the bag. It was much bigger than his pocket! Now, he could bring home all the pinecones, rocks, and chestnuts he could carry.

Skipping home, he called out to his mother. "Mom, look what I found!"

"Not again," his mother squeaked. "I told you to stop picking stuff up!" But then she saw the old, ugly bag in his paws. Thinking it was just a worthless, old rag, she told Jasper he could keep it.

Jasper carried around the bag for the rest of his days. The bag was never empty; even in the bleakest of times, Jasper always found nuts and seeds and berries. Even in the coldest of winters, he found sweet berries blooming on bushes. The bag never provided gold or diamonds, but it always ensured a full tummy for Jasper—and his entire village—for many, many years to come. Jasper called the bag his greatest treasure, and it was. A gift from the fairies to a little mouse who did the right thing and gave back what was not his to claim.

When Jasper died, the other mice wrapped his body in the old, tattered bag.

"He sure loved this thing. Why, we don't know," they squeaked. "It is so old and ratty and dirty."

"He would have wanted us to bury him with it," they sighed. "Plus, it's a way to get rid of it," they added. They certainly had no use for the decrepit piece of cloth.

On Jasper's grave, a tiny sapling grew bearing golden seed pods that sparkled in the sun. The village named it "Jasper's Tree." Legend says that fairies bury their treasure on this site, but woe to the thief who tries to steal it for his own.

Just Look at the Sky

Once, there lived a tiny rat named Oliver. Oliver loved nature; he especially liked to sleep outside under the stars. His mom would call him in when the sky turned dark, but Oliver always said, "Just a bit longer, Mom. I can see the Big Dipper now, and my friends, the fireflies and the crickets, are out." And Oliver's mom would smile and say, "All right, son, just stay close to the burrow opening, and call if you need anything."

Oliver loved the night—the tiny night insects that sang, the owls that hooted, the misty fog that settled close to the woodland ground. But there were dangers in the night, and Oliver knew he had to keep very quiet and still; rustling sounds through the hedgerows meant larger beings were also roaming in the dark. He loved listening to hoots and howls, but he would listen very quietly, never letting the creatures that made them know he was about.

One night, a strange noise, really a cry, startled Oliver. Disobeying his mom's rule, he strayed a bit farther through the hedgerow and came upon a very small baby rat. Now, Oliver wasn't full grown yet, but he was much bigger than this tiny orphan.

"Where are your parents?" Oliver asked.

The baby sniffled and shook his head. "I don't know. There was a very large shadow, and then Mama was gone."

Oliver saw a tiny bit of blood on the baby's rear leg. "You need help," he squeaked.

Oliver thought for a moment.....what should he do? He couldn't leave this little baby out in the night by himself, so Oliver gently picked him up in his paws and took him home to his own mama.

"What on earth??" Mama squeaked. "Why, you are no bigger than a peanut! What are you doing out here by yourself?"

Oliver told Mama what the little rat had said, and Mama gave the baby a gentle squeeze. "You're safe now, little one," she whispered. "Come, let's give you a nice warm blanket and some cookie crumbs. Do you have a name?"

"My mama called me Sunny," he squeaked.

"Well, Sunny, you can stay with us," she whispered with a smile. She gently licked his wound with her soft tongue and cleaned all the dirt away.

The baby grew very quickly. Soon, he was following Oliver around constantly, just like a little brother. He would beg to sleep outside with Oliver, but Mama protested, saying he was still too little. Besides, his leg had not fully healed, and he could not run as quickly if another animal chased him.

But one night, the little baby crept outside anyway to find his brother. "Oliver, Oliver," he squeaked. But Oliver did not answer. Soon, the baby was lost in the hedgerow.

It was very, very late when Oliver came inside to sleep and noticed his brother's side of the bed was empty. "Mama, Mama, where is Sunny?"

Mama went searching frantically. She searched where the cookies were kept, but he wasn't there. She searched every corner, under all the blankets, and called his name in the night. "Oh no!" she cried.

Oliver dashed out. No one knew the night like Oliver. "I will find him, Mama. Don't worry," he assured his mom, though he was more than a bit worried.

Oliver searched the hedgerows. He asked the crickets and the fireflies if they had seen a little rat. He knocked on other rat burrow doors, even though some were not too happy about being awakened in the middle of the night.

"Please, has anyone seen my brother? He has a wounded leg and is out here in the night all alone."

"Well, wasn't your mother watching him?" they criticized. "It's too dangerous out there. We will look in the morning." They slammed their burrow doors shut.

Oliver was dismayed at the negative comments other rats spoke about his mom. "She's the best mom in the world!" he answered, and he went on searching. Finally, he heard a faint squeak.

"Sunny, Sunny, is that you?"

"Oliver, down here." The tiny rat had fallen down a deep hole. "I cannot climb out. My leg is very sore. I just wanted to stay outside with you. Please don't be mad, Oliver."

Oliver wasn't mad; he was just very scared and worried. A large animal could reach his paw down that hole and scoop up Sunny in a minute. First, he tried to dig around the hole, but that made things worse. More dirt came tumbling down on his brother's head.

"I am going to place this branch above the hole so you will be safe." Oliver laid an evergreen branch over the spot and looked up at the sky. He knew all the stars and pictures in the sky. He looked above so he would know exactly where his brother waited. "Stay very quiet," Oliver said reassuringly. "I will get Mama." And off he ran.

Oliver and Mama ran back. It was very dark and foggy, and Mama was worried about the two of them getting lost or worse.

"Don't worry, Mama," Oliver said. "I know the sky. I know the stars. You just have to look at the sky to know where we are. There are pictures in the sky, Mama. Look, I see the Big Dog, the Small Dog, the Lion."

Mama looked in wonder at her son, her eyes gazing in awe as he pointed his paw in all directions toward the stars. And Oliver *did* know where they were. He guided his mother to the very spot Sunny waited. Mama dug a tunnel alongside and reached the baby in no time. She led him to safety above ground and hugged him tightly.

"I am sorry, Mama," the baby squeaked.

Oliver hugged his brother and gave a huge rat sigh of relief. Mama scooped Sunny in her paws, and the three hurried home. By now, the morning sun was beginning to rise on the horizon.

"You saved him, Mama," Oliver cried.

"No, you saved him, Oliver. Without you, I would never have found his spot in the forest. Your wise eyes know the sky and the stars. *You* found him."

The little family of three slept all day. They awoke early evening, and Mama said, "Let's all go outside and look at the stars."

So, she wrapped both her babies in warm blankets, took their paws, and together they watched the night sky. Mama carried a bag of cookie crumbs for snacks. Oliver told them all the stories that the crickets and fireflies and other night creatures had told him. He pointed to all the pictures in the night sky. He told them to make a wish when they saw a shooting star.

"I have no need of wishes," Mama cried. "My wishes are right beside me."

And as the little rat family watched, a bright shooting star blazed across the dark sky.

Hats and Homes

In a small English village in the Lake District, there lived a kindly old woman in a humble cottage surrounded by fields and woodlands. Maggie loved the countryside, the lakes, and the wildlife that chirped and squeaked and ran through the fields. And she loved her garden. Each day, you could find her among the flower patches. Not proper English ones, but a jumble of tall wildflowers and berries and grasses that nourished all who came.

And come they did. Birds and moles and badgers and hedgehogs, foxes and squirrels and butterflies ran and flew among the colors. There were wild English roses. Not the kind the grocer carried that had no smell. These were fragrant blossoms that filled the air, along with English lavender that the woman collected and dried, tied in bunches, and brought to market to sell.

Everyone in the village knew which market stall belonged to her. Maggie always wore a wide-brimmed straw hat. She had a collection of hats, in all colors, trimmed with colorful scarves and ribbons. Nowadays, most people wear baseball caps. Not many still wear wide-brimmed country hats, but the old woman loved them. If you spotted one, most likely it was at Maggie's garden stand. Bunches of lavender, homemade honey from her hives, and fresh-cut bouquets of colorful wildflowers adorned the stall. People in the village loved her.

One morning, on an extremely blustery day, Maggie was carrying a bunch of bouquets to market. A huge gust of wind came and blew her large hat straight into the air! She tried to catch it, but it flew higher and higher, straight across the field to the edge of the woodland.

"Oh my," she cried. "I will have to go looking tomorrow. It's nearly noon, and the market has opened by now." And so off she went, hatless. Everyone along the way stopped her and asked, "Where's your hat, Maggie?" At the end of the day, she went home, searching the faraway field for any glimpse of pink, the color of her favorite straw hat.

The next morning, Maggie set out on her straw hat quest. She donned her wellies, put on another straw hat (that she tied under her chin with a long scarf), and went walking across the field, her faithful terrier Lucy alongside. She walked all the way to the edge of the woodland and, just as she was about to turn around for home empty-handed, she spotted the pink hat upside down on the ground. Lucy let out a bark.

"My hat!" Maggie exclaimed, so happy to find it. But when she looked down to reach for it, she discovered a startling surprise. There, snuggled inside the hat, with just a bit of pink peeking out, was a trio of baby bunnies. "Well, I guess this is your home now," Maggie smiled. "Come, Lucy. Let's go home. Keep them safe, my favorite pink hat," she whispered to the heavens.

Maggie walked each day, checking on the babies. As they grew, they started to roam, but they always returned to the safety of the straw hat. One day, though, it was empty. The pink hat lay forlorn, now tattered and dirty on the ground. "Well," whispered Maggie, "perhaps someone else will find you."

And find the hat they did. It became home to a nest of wild sparrows for a while. Next, a little squirrel carried it up a tree where it sat among the branches for the entire winter, offering shelter amidst the cold and windy moors.

Years passed, and Maggie would sometimes leave hats out in the tall grasses. Little ones always found them and made the hats their homes. Tiny dormice loved the hats; they snuggled inside, sheltered from the harsh English weather.

Maggie had so many hats, too many to possibly wear. So, she shared with all the little beings she loved. She made friendly scarecrows in her garden and topped them with yellow and blue and green straw hats. The scarecrows never shooed the birds away, and the hats often disappeared from the tops of their heads. Many crow families nestled their young inside them.

Lucy grew old, and when Maggie laid her to rest, she placed her tiny body inside a warm blanket. Then, Maggie nestled her dear friend in her largest and most beautiful straw bonnet, in the prettiest spot within her garden.

When Maggie passed away, her village friends found a little note tucked among her remaining pile of straw hats. The instructions read, *Wait for a very windy day and toss these in the air.* Her friends were perplexed, but they granted Maggie's wish.

On a blustery March morning, they gathered outside her cottage door, each with a big straw hat in hand. Together, they said a tearful goodbye to Maggie and let the wind carry the wide brims into the air. They watched them sail across the fields and woodlands.

Maggie's spirit was watching and smiling. And she didn't watch alone—the robins, mice, bunnies, and squirrels all sang and chirped a "thank you" to their kind and caring friend. And perhaps a tiny bark filled the air, as well.

Years passed. Those of the old generation always remembered the kind village woman with the large straw hats. The cottage still stands. A young woman lovingly tends the garden now, dressed in overalls and a baseball cap. She gathers the English lavender in bundles and takes them to market each Saturday. She makes homemade jams and scented creams with English rose petals. She sells baseball caps with the logo "*Jenny's Farm*" printed on their brims. She decorates scarecrows with baseball caps instead of straw hats. And sometimes, they disappear.

"Must be the English wind. It's brutal out here," she whispers to herself.

Must be....................

The Lantern

Zahar lived in a village of winds that swirled with sand and spices. With long, beautiful, black hair and eyes as dark as the night sky, Zahar lived alone in one of the poor hovels of the village. Her mother had died of sickness years before, and Zahar had managed to survive by searching the shores for shipwreck debris.

Ships passed in and out of the harbor many times during the week, carrying spices valued more than the poor people of Zahar's village. In return, they carried items for the wealthy, to be sold in bazaars and market stalls for those with coins that jingled in their robes.

One early morning, the shipwreck bell rang throughout the land. The bell was the signal to hurry down to the shoreline and search the rocks for anything of value. Zahar ran. Most were looking down in the sands, sifting for coins or rings or silver that gleamed in the sun's rays. But Zahar heard a strange sound. A call for help screeched through the palms overhead, and Zahar's dark eyes squinted in the sunlight to see a tiny monkey cowering in the fronds.

Zahar was a kind soul. She barely had bread to fill her own hungry stomach, but she always shared with the doves (who hid from individuals wishing to cage them for the market stalls).

"Little one, where did you come from?" Zahar asked the monkey.

The monkey saw kindness in her eyes and trusted enough to climb down into her arms.

"Oh, you have been hurt!" she cried, gesturing to a cut sustained on the sharp shoreline rocks. "Come, I will help you."

And so, she bundled the tiny monkey inside her worn satchel and hurried home to her humble hut. She washed the monkey's wound and gave him some broth she had simmering on her hearth.

"I am Karim."

Startled, Zahar looked around, expecting an intruder had followed her home. Her village was not a safe place for an orphaned girl.

Again, the voice repeated, "I am Karim. Thank you for your kindness."

Zahar saw that the voice belonged to the tiny primate. "You can talk!" she gasped.

"Please do not be frightened. I need your help. Please help me!" Karim pleaded.

"I....I don't know..." Zahar started to stutter.

Karim continued with his plea. "I must find my master's lantern. It drifted on the tide, and I lost sight of it. I am tied to the lantern. Without it, I will die."

Zahar did not understand. She did not understand any of this. Perhaps she was dreaming. But no, it was morning. The sun was glinting through her tiny doorway. The fire was simmering broth. There was a monkey sitting there, talking.

"Please," Karim pleaded. "We must find it before someone else does. Without my jinn, I will die!"

Now, Zahar's mother had told her bedtime tales of jinns and magic. Lamps that could grant wishes, lamps that could bring fortune or doom. Zahar's land was a land that believed in jinns.

"I will help you," she answered.

Scooping Karim up inside her satchel, she hurried down to the shoreline. The searchers were all gone; any goods had already been claimed. With a heavy heart, Zahar told Karim that the lamp was probably gone and on its way to the marketplace by now.

"I have no money to buy such a gift. Your lantern must be beautiful," she exclaimed.

"No," Karim replied. "It is old and tarnished and dented, valuable only to the smelter's furnace for its metal."

Zahar knew where the smelter's shop was located, and the two of them set off on their quest for the lantern. Sure enough, high atop the smelter's wagon sat the dented lantern on a pile of scrap metal from the ship.

The smelter's donkey brayed as Zahar and Karim stepped closer. "Who's there? Who is trying to steal my metal?" the smelter cried, running out of his shop.

"Hurry, Karim! Hide in my satchel," she whispered with fright.

Turning to the smelter, Zahar screamed, "Please, sir, I mean no harm!"

"Please," Zahar again cried, knowing that stealing was punishable by death in her village.

"What do you want?" the smelter yelled.

"The old lantern, sir. May I have it?" Zahar pleaded.

"I don't give things away!!" the smelter screamed. "You have coins?" he angrily asked.

"No," Zahar cried.

"Then go home!"

Zahar's eyes filled with tears as she turned away.

"Wait," the smelter smirked. "That is a lovely head scarf. My wife would surely love to have it."

"But my mother embroidered this scarf for me. It is all I have left of her."

"The scarf for the lantern. Yes or no?" the unkind merchant repeated.

"I must cover my hair. I have nothing else, and the village will punish me if they see me without my head scarf. Please, have mercy," Zahar cried.

"Here," the merchant scowled, throwing a dirty, old, black rag to Zahar. "Here is your head scarf. Now give me yours!"

The merchant threw the old lantern to her feet, making a new dent in its side. With tears falling to the sand, Zahar picked up the lantern, wrapped her beautiful locks with the dirty rag, and went home. She placed the lantern down by the fire as the monkey watched her tear-streaked face glow in the flame's light.

"Thank you, Zahar," he whispered as his paws rubbed the lantern's side. Instantly, a huge puff of smoke filled the room, forming into the shape of a handsome jinn. He wore a jewel-encrusted turban and silk pointed sandals on his feet. His vest was embroidered with lovely designs, and tassels hung from the waistband of his pants.

"Well, Karim. It seems you have found me to live another day," he laughed. "It seems you have also found another owner of this lantern."

Karim pleaded, "Please, master. She is only an innocent, kind soul. Do not trap her with wishes."

The jinn smiled. "That is the way of the land, my Karim. The one who owns the lantern owns the wishes," he replied.

"Now, Zahar, you have three wishes. Use them wisely," he laughed.

"No, Zahar, don't. Throw the lantern in the flames!" Karim pleaded.

But Zahar's dark eyes were mesmerized by the jinn. She held the lantern in her hands and said, "I wish to free Karim."

With a second caress of the lantern, she said, "I wish to find my own true love."

With that wish, Karim disappeared in a whirl of smoke, and a handsome, young man stood by the fire, his eyes as dark as the night sky.

"So, you have fallen in love, Karim," the jinn smirked.

Zahar looked upon the dark eyes of the young man and instantly returned his love.

"So unfortunate," the jinn spoke. "To find love and lose it so quickly."

Karim lowered his head in sorrow. Once severed, the curse of the jinn meant death for Karim. Within moments, he slumped to the ground, whispering his last words, "I love you, Zahar."

"No!!!" Zahar cried.

"You have one more wish, Zahar. Wealth, jewels, a ship to take you around the world. Anything is at your beck and call. What will it be?" the jinn asked.

"I wish to find my own true love," she repeated.

"But..." the jinn hesitated. "That is a wish granted only by......Do you know what this means, foolish girl?" The jinn glowered, his eyes aglow with the hearth flames.

With his words, Zahar sank to the ground and closed her tear-filled eyes.

"Stupid girl," said the jinn. "You could have had the world, and you chose death."

Folklore tells a tale of two spectral doves who soar above the rocks, always together, with beautiful eyes as dark as the night sky. Some claim to have seen their nest high above the rocks in a place too steep for man to climb. A beautiful, embroidered scarf, woven with loving care, is said to be entwined through the palm fronds of the nest—a head scarf carried off in the beak of a dove in the middle of the night from a smelter's open window.

The lantern and its jinn? Well, that is a bedtime story for another night.

Mourning and Fire

Once upon a time, in a village far isolated in the woods, there lived a witch named Carmella and her little mouse. The witch loved this tiny companion, and the feelings were returned by this palm-sized bundle of fur. Now, he was a special mouse, as well; he could speak. His name was Magellan.

People in the village hated witches, and they hated mice, too. They blamed both for illness and called them pests that needed to be exterminated. And yet, villagers sought the witch's help when all other methods of healing failed.

Carmella never harmed anyone. She kept a solitary life among the creatures of the forest. Each season, with her tiny companion in her large apron pocket, the witch would roam the forest, picking acorns and weeds and bits of bark for all her herbal tisanes. Her pockets held broken bird eggs and hag stones and witch burrs, along with dried rose hips and milkweed pods.

One day, the little mouse spotted a beautiful butterfly cocoon that hung from a branch. He squeaked and pointed his paw to the lovely green bundle that looked like it had been sprinkled with gold.

"Ah," the witch grinned. "That is indeed a treasure. Within it sleeps a beautiful butterfly, so kingly that his name is monarch. One day, he will spread his lovely orange and black wings and fly a great distance home."

The mouse wondered how his friend could know all things. "Carmella, where did you find me?" he asked one brisk morning on their walk. "Was I like an acorn you found and put in your pocket?"

"Yes, you were the best treasure I ever found," Carmella answered. "More lovely than any stone, flower, or pinecone in this wood," she smiled.

Magellan squeaked with approval. Carmella was more than a friend; she was his mom. When his tummy ached, she brewed him delicious chamomile tea. When his teeth ached, she poured hot water over willow bark and let it simmer until cool enough for him to sip.

He wondered why none of the other villagers liked her or him for that matter. When anyone came to her dwelling, Carmella told him to hide. "Never let anyone know you can speak," she warned. "They will not understand, and what they don't understand, they kill," she whispered with such sadness in her eyes.

Each day, the pair would pass the beautiful cocoon hanging in the tree. "Is the King ready?" Magellan asked.

"Not yet, but soon," she answered with a smile. "Let us leave him to sleep for now. Come, we have much to look for today. There is a young woman in the village with a baby due soon. She will come to our door for help. I must find wild raspberries."

Together, they walked, searching the forest floor until they came upon a wild raspberry bush. Magellan took so many mouthfuls of the delicious berry, his whole face was soon stained red. With enough to make a tea, Carmella scooped up the tiny mouse, wiped his mouth on her apron, and tucked him inside her pocket. They headed home, and sure enough, that evening, a frantic knock came upon the witch's door.

"Please help me! The pain is unbearable," cried the young woman, hunched over in agony. "Something is very wrong. Please help me!!" she cried.

Carmella took the girl, braced her against her arm, and led her inside her cottage. She urged the young woman to sip the raspberry tea, and she made a soft bed with clean linens washed in the nearby stream. "Relax and let the tea work its magick," she whispered.

There were twins born that night. Only one survived.

In the morning, a harsh knock rapped on Carmella's door. "Where is my wife, witch?" the man yelled.

Carmella looked at Magellan, and the little, trembling mouse hid in a dark corner. "She is in here, resting. You have a beautiful, little daughter. Come see," Carmella replied.

The man came to his wife's bed and saw a tiny bundle in her arms. Then, he spotted a tiny bundle in a basket on the floor.

"I am sorry," Carmella said. "There were two, a boy and a girl. The boy was still at birth."

The man's eyes filled with fury. "You took my son, witch! You will pay for this!!" And without a word of comfort for his wife, he raced out of the cottage like a madman.

"Mama, what is happening?" the little mouse asked, shaking with fear. "You only tried to help her. You saved the baby," he questioned.

Without her help, both mother and daughter would surely have died. But the villagers would not see it this way. Carmella knew what was coming. She whispered to the resting mother that all would be okay, that her husband would return for her. Carmella then scooped up the tiny mouse in her pocket and ran inside the deep forest.

Magellan could feel Carmella's pounding heart, and his began to beat in time with hers. They reached the tree where the King slept.

"It is time," she whispered to the beautiful cocoon.

Magellan watched as the cocoon spread open and lovely orange and black wings spread apart.

"Do not be afraid, my son," she told the little mouse. "He is one of us. Throughout centuries, we have traveled great distances to escape the fear of those who do not understand. Now, we will join him."

Magellan felt a strange sensation pass over his whiskers, down to his paws and tummy. He felt something strange on his back. Mama was gone, too.

"Mama, Mama, where are you?" he cried.

"Look up, son." The mouse saw two monarch butterflies, their orange and black wings fluttering in the morning breeze. Then, he felt the breeze lifting his tiny body in the air. He felt the flutter of wings, his own wings, take him to the sky.

The three of them flew, high above the trees, high above the raspberries and roses and willows. They flew to the cottage and saw a group of men coming closer with lighted torches. Following behind, he saw the angry man yelling at them. But they were too filled with rage to hear. They ran ahead, hatred in their eyes and loud voices yelling, "The witch will die!"

"Mama! Mama!" Magellan cried.

"Come, my son. We have miles and miles to journey before we sleep."

The man reached the mob too late. He was tired from running to the village to incite this mob; their feet were faster and reached the cottage several minutes before his. The torches reached the thatch roof. It took mere seconds for the entire cottage to be engulfed in flames. The men looked over at the man's face, now filled with fright.

"You fools!" he shouted. "My wife was inside!!" The grief-stricken man slumped down to the ground, his hands covering his face.

From a pine branch high above the flames, three butterflies watched. Their wings were forever marked with black and orange, for centuries of mourning and fire.

The Book Witch

Once upon a time, there lived a very kind witch. Now this was no ordinary witch. She possessed special magick, the magick of words. At a time when very few knew how to read, Libby possessed this gift. She knew words; she knew books; she knew stories that traveled through time and faraway lands.

Owning books was a rare privilege for both humans and woodland dwellers in those times. Not many had ever laid eyes on the wavy lines that spoke from pages. Libby had a small, ivy-covered cottage overflowing with books and stories. Her parents had been the keepers of books, the book witches of her country. Their magick was kept in the pages of words.

Most witches used them for good, a few for evil. Libby was good. Her books told only stories that filled minds with wonder. So many stories, but so little room; Libby was running out of places to keep her treasures and worried who might be the keeper of stories once she was gone.

Each afternoon, Libby sat on the trunk of a massive willow tree and read in the sunlight. Soon, all the creatures of the forest would sit by her side and listen to her tell them tales of pirates and mermaids and wizards and dragons that breathed fire. She told them how the willow and other trees gave their spirits in pages upon which magick words spoke. Together, they would sit until the sun lowered her head and it grew too dark to read.

All the little animals loved her stories and asked if she might teach them to read, as well. They had very sharp eyes and could see the print long after Libby's vision failed in the fading light. So, Libby agreed to give reading lessons to all her friends. The foxes and raccoons were quick learners; soon, they were reciting the alphabet and learning short words. The birds, though, had short attention spans; they would flutter their wings and look off toward the sky. They took longer to learn, but Libby was a kind and patient teacher. Ferdinand Fox was her favorite student. He always hungered for the next adventure or the next historical tale of times long past in the forest.

Through the years, Libby taught generations of forest dwellers the gift of reading. When she grew old and frail and could not sit comfortably on the willow for long periods of time, the animals read to her at her bedside.

One day, Libby closed her eyes in peace as Ferdinand Fox read her a beautiful poetry passage. "Thank you," she whispered with a fading smile on her face. "Make my home a place of magick," she sighed. "Make it a place where all my books can be taken home, read, and returned for another to enjoy."

"I promise, Libby," Ferdinand softly answered with a tearful howl.

Ferdinand kept his promise. Libby's home was indeed a magical place, a place with tiny rooms where pirates, fairies, wizards, trolls, kings, queens, and princesses dwelled. Generations learned the magic of reading because of her kindness. A library came to be because a loving witch sat on a willow tree in the sunlight one day with a storybook in her hand.

Ferdinand became the next keeper of books, and so it followed that all his children, and their children after, became the librarians of a special place of magick in the woods. Huge willows grew along the path, and tiny benches beckoned minds to sit and read and dream.

A special author shelf held the most prized piece in the library's collection: *Libby the Book Witch* by Ferdinand Fox.

Once upon a time, long, long ago, there lived a village of warriors. They knew battle; they pillaged neighboring villages, and they caused suffering and death unheralded before their time. Now, in their village lived a kind witch. She was persecuted for showing kindness to those wounded or left without family; she was tortured and imprisoned in the warrior king's castle.

The king's son was too sickly to be a warrior. An embarrassment to his father, he was assigned the duty of prison guard. With little food or comforts to give, he did his best to make the lives of those in his care a bit less painful. But conditions were so harsh, even his kindness mattered not. His dark, piercing eyes filled with sorrow as he watched the endless suffering, all at his father's hands.

The witch was left to wallow in darkness and filth for years, her only companions being the poor souls imprisoned and held captive as spoils of war. The morsels of stale bread the prince could sneak away from his father's kitchen could only lengthen the time of her suffering.

The prince himself became much sicker in the dank prison air. His father hardly uttered a sigh of grief or worry.

His other sons were strong warriors; his feeble son was just another captive soul left to die.

Eventually, the unhealthy conditions caused the witch to become extremely ill. On her deathbed, she vowed revenge on all those who found war to be the way of life. *From this day forward*, she whispered…

All who sought war in my village will become the tools of such cruelty.

You shall be used as instruments of destruction, and countless numbers of your generations will suffer and die at the hands of others in battle.

You will never forget your closeness to man; you will crave his companionship and be loyal slaves in battle.

Your names will not be remembered. Your deaths will not be mourned.

Very few of you will escape imprisonment. Those who do will roam wild in the hillsides—forever fearful of being captured—and fulfill the needs of those who you once were.

They will try to break some of you; most will fall and do their bidding.

Some will race until their last heartbeats as entertainment.

Some will carry heavy burdens into difficult terrain.

Most will carry warriors until their legs give out from under them, riddled with bullets and cannon fire.

This, I promise.

And with that, she let out her final sigh.

Suddenly, a thunderous clattering of hoof beats stormed through the prison. Hundreds of horses, their nostrils flared with fear, broke down the gates and fled into the fields. Most captive prisoners ran for their lives, reaching neighboring villages and telling them of the strange creatures that filled the warrior king's land.

One horse, a horse with flowing black mane and eyes that reached deep within his soul, lingered by the prison door of the witch. Those prisoners who stayed behind to guard the witch's body placed her upon this steed's back. They walked beside him as he gently carried the witch back to the fields of her humble cottage. The fellow prisoners buried her among the wildflowers as the stallion lowered his head in mourning, his eyes filled with sorrow.

The wars continued, as is the way of man. But now, the way of war had changed. Large, hooved creatures carried the warriors. Countless died in agony, their bodies left to rot in the fields.

Only a few refused to yield and became wild and free. And legend says, a large, beautiful black stallion with piercing eyes led them into the sheltered woods to live in peace.

Once upon a time, there was a snow-capped mountain village where families of elves lived. Now, elves are very tiny, you see, so they have teeny mice for pets. They walk them with tiny cords for leashes and give them supper in bowls made from hollowed out acorns. Elf moms knit tiny boots for mouse paws so the snow won't freeze their little toes. The sound of squeaks, not barks, fill the air when elf friends come to call.

Christmas in the village was always a grand affair. Well, you know, it had to be with elves. Each elf house was decorated with woodland garlands, and each elf parlor proudly displayed a large branch that was adorned with cookies and tinsel and glowing candles.

In this village, there stood a large snowman. Well, he was about two feet tall, large by elf standards. The elf children had taken much care in sculpting him. Two branches served as his arms. (Mischievous little mice tried to drag them away as playing sticks, but they were much too cumbersome.)

Sometimes, while elf children slept, pet mice crawled out of the bed covers and crept away to play under the moon and stars. On one of these nights, they heard a soft whisper in the moonlight.

"Hello, friends." The words carried on the winter wind.

"Who is that?" one of the mice squeaked, his voice cracking with fright.

"Don't be afraid. It's me, the snowman," the voice answered.

"Snowmen can't talk," one of the mice squeaked.

"Well, I can," boasted the snow-covered figure. "I am a very old snowman. My snow is from the ancient glaciers that formed this mountain. I hold the wisdom of generations of elf villages and centuries of elf stories."

The tiny mice eyes grew twice as large. "Stories? Can you tell us some?" they squeaked. (Mice love stories, you see. Next to fetching sticks and having furry heads petted, listening to stories is something all baby mice learn to love from the time they can let out their first squeaks.)

"Why, yes," the snowman answered. "But I ask one wish in return."

"What wish?" questioned one of the mice hesitantly.

"Don't fret. It's not a bad wish. In fact, it's a very nice one. You see, all these Christmases, I have watched families bring in fir branches and make them sparkle. My branches are always dry and brittle and barren. How I wish I could sparkle for Christmas, just once!"

The mice squeaked and chattered amongst themselves, nodding their furry mice heads and glancing back and forth every now and then to the snowman.

"It's a deal," the largest mouse squeaked.

There wasn't much time before the children stirred in their beds and came calling their pets to come inside. The mice scurried to and fro, back to each of their homes, carting off a bit of tinsel and cookie in their paws. They scampered in the snow to find berries and acorns, and one carried off a bit of red embroidery thread from a mother elf's basket. They chewed teeny holes in the acorns and berries. Together, they worked and worked, tossing and threading, and when they were finished, the snowman's arms were sparkling.

Tiny icicles glistened on the snowman's cheeks as he looked upon his Christmas arms. "Thank you, dear mice. You have granted a very old snowman's one wish."

The dawn was gently breaking; the mice had to hurry home. "Remember your promise," they squeaked. "We will come for our stories tomorrow night." And with that, they squeaked away to squeeze back into the cracks and holes of elf homes to snuggle to sleep for the day.

That morning, elf children jumped out of their tiny beds and raced to their Christmas trees and stockings. It was Christmas, you see, and elves always make plenty of presents for their little ones.

There was so much commotion that the mice couldn't get a good hour's rest. They were awakened by their elf children to play with new balls and toys in the snow.

"Be careful outside," elf parents warned. "There was an avalanche at the base of the snow mountain very early this morning. Your beautiful snowman was covered. You will have to make another one for Christmas."

"What!!!" the mice squeaked. "Our snowman? Our stories?"

It was true. When the elf children took them outside to play, the mice looked over to the spot where the snowman had stood. Now, only a large pile of snow remained. Old snow from the mountain cap. Ancient snow, from a long-ago glacier. Sparkling in the morning sun, watching, listening for more stories, stories that held time in each ice crystal.

The mice had their story, too, though perhaps they did not realize it at the time. A story they would pass on to each of their children. A story about the night a friend asked to have just one special Christmas.

www.ingramcontent.com/pod-product-compliance
Lightning Source LLC
LaVergne TN
LVHW090529110826
845146LV00003B/1030

* 9 7 9 8 2 3 4 0 1 8 5 5 7 *